Praise for

Akimbo

A Book Sense Children's Pick

"Akimbo is a very brave little boy who keeps his wits about him even when he's being stalked by a rhino."
—*The New York Times Book Review*

"Satisfying page-turners that celebrate kids' curiosity, love of adventure, and capacity to care for the world they inhabit." —*Parenting* magazine

"The tale's brevity, Smith's concise writing and Pham's evocative full-page half-tone illustrations make this an attractive choice for reluctant readers."
—*Publishers Weekly*

"Akimbo emerges as a brave, caring protagonist who faces dilemmas and danger in the service of the animals and people he loves." —*Booklist*

"The African setting, dramatic full-page pencil illustrations, and the animal facts woven into the stories are sure to capture young readers." —*SLJ*

"[These] gently told yet exciting stories reveal another side of McCall Smith's love for Africa, championing the importance of wild animals amid threats to their survival." —*Chicago Sun-Times*

"Smith captures the essence of his beloved Africa in the same manner as that which has made his adult 'No. 1 Ladies' Detective Agency' series so popular."
—*Monterey County Herald*

ALEXANDER McCALL SMITH

AKIMBO and the SNAKES

BURROWS MEDIA CENTER

ILLUSTRATED BY LeUyen Pham

BLOOMSBURY
CHILDREN'S
BOOKS

Published by Bloomsbury U.S.A. Children's Books
175 Fifth Avenue, New York, NY 10010

The Library of Congress has cataloged the hardcover edition as follows:
McCall Smith, Alexander.
Akimbo and the snakes / by Alexander McCall Smith ;
illustrations by LeUyen Pham.—1st U.S. ed.
p.   cm.
Summary: On a trip to the snake park with his uncle Peter, Akimbo has an
adventure involving a deadly green mamba snake.
ISBN-13: 978-1-58234-705-9 • ISBN-10: 1-58234-705-0 (hardcover)
[1. Snakes—Fiction. 2. Mambas—Fiction. 3. Africa—Fiction.]
I. Pham, LeUyen, ill. II. Title.
PZ7.M47833755Ap 2006   [Fic]—dc22   2006006947

ISBN-13: 978-1-59990-034-6 • ISBN-10: 1-59990-034-3 (paperback)

The author's royalties from this book are being donated to
The Lady Khama Trust in Botswana for charitable purposes
connected with the welfare of children.

Typeset by Westchester Book Composition
Printed in the U.S.A. by Worzalla
3 5 7 9 10 8 6 4 2

All papers used by Bloomsbury U.S.A. are natural, recyclable products made
from wood grown in well-managed forests. The manufacturing processes
conform to the environmental regulations of the country of origin.

FOR BENJAMIN, CAROLYN, AND ERIC

CONTENTS

An Exciting Invitation

Akimbo was very proud of his uncle Peter, although he hardly ever saw him. Once or twice a year, though, Uncle Peter would make the journey out to the great game reserve where his brother, Akimbo's father, was the head ranger. These visits would always start the same way. Uncle Peter and Akimbo's father would sit down on the veranda and talk about family matters until the sun burnt down behind the hills and the African night filled with stars.

The following morning, though, would be Akimbo's special time, and Uncle Peter would sit with his nephew and tell him stories about his job, which to Akimbo seemed to be just about the most exciting job imaginable.

Uncle Peter ran a snake park! Akimbo had seen photographs of the park and wanted to visit it for a long time. He always loved to hear Uncle Peter talk about the snakes he had caught and what happened to them. Sometimes the snakes died or escaped or hatched eggs, and all these events struck Akimbo as being very interesting and exciting. He had asked more than once whether it would be possible for him to visit his uncle and see the snake park, but he had always been told he would have to wait until he was a bit older.

At last the day came when, at the end of one of Uncle Peter's visits, it was agreed that Akimbo could go to stay with his uncle during the next school vacation.

"I'll meet you off the bus," said Uncle Peter. "And you can spend three or four weeks with us. Your parents have agreed. Would you like that?"

"I'd love it," said Akimbo.

"You'll have to help out, though," Uncle Peter went on.

Akimbo's face beamed with pleasure at the thought. "You mean, help out with the snakes?" he asked.

Uncle Peter nodded. "Yes," he said. "Think of it as a working vacation."

Akimbo was delighted. Over the next month, scarcely a day went past when he did not dream about the visit that lay ahead of him. Finally the day of his departure arrived, and his father took him to meet the bus that would take him off to Uncle Peter's town.

"Be careful," urged Akimbo's father. "And remember to write a letter to your mother."

Akimbo promised that he would. As the bus drew noisily away, he put his hand out of the window and waved cheerfully to his father. His father waved back, and then, in a cloud of dust and with a raucous hooting of the horn, the bus was on its way.

The journey was very uncomfortable. Even with all the windows open, the bus was hot and stuffy. A woman sitting next to Akimbo gave him a roasted maize cob and let him drink from her bottle of water, but before

long Akimbo began to feel hungry and thirsty again and longed for the journey to end.

They passed through villages and small towns, picking up and dropping off passengers here and there. People boarded with baskets of chickens, which squealed and clucked as they felt the unfamiliar motion of the bus. A man boarded with a dog tied to a piece of string, and Akimbo thought he had never seen such a miserable-looking animal.

It was nighttime before they arrived in Uncle Peter's town. Akimbo had dozed off, and was woken up by the lights. As the bus drew up to its stop, and the passengers all started to jostle their way out, Akimbo caught a glimpse of Uncle Peter waiting for him. It was a welcome sight in a strange town, and soon he was loading his case into the back of his Uncle's truck.

"You look hungry," said Uncle Peter, as he steered the truck through the traffic. "I'll stop at a stall."

Soon Akimbo was tucking into a delicious thick iced roll and drinking from a cold bottle of soda. He felt immediately better, and the discomfort of the journey seemed now to be a thing of the past.

"I think you should go to bed the moment we get to my house," said Uncle Peter. "You want to be fresh for tomorrow, don't you?"

Akimbo nodded. Tomorrow he would see the snake park. Perhaps Uncle Peter would let him handle a snake. Perhaps something exciting would happen. He would have to wait and see.

MILKING TIME

kimbo awoke early the next morning. By the time Uncle Peter emerged from his bedroom, he was already sitting at the kitchen table, fully dressed.

Uncle Peter laughed to see his nephew ready so early. "I can tell you can't wait to get going," he said.

Akimbo nodded. "I've been looking forward to this day for a long time."

Uncle Peter cut several pieces of bread and spread them thickly with margarine and jam. This, together with a hot mug of tea, was Akimbo's breakfast, which he ate eagerly.

"You must have seen quite a few snakes before," Uncle Peter said. "Living out at the game park, you could hardly miss them."

"Yes," said Akimbo. "But I've not had the chance to look at them closely. They're usually slithering away under a bush or into a hole."

Uncle Peter nodded. "That's why snake parks are so important," he said. "People can see snakes at close quarters. They can learn all about them."

They finished breakfast and set off for the snake park in Uncle Peter's truck. It was just outside the town, and the journey took a little while, but at last they were there. Akimbo recognized it from the photographs and felt great pride when he saw his uncle's name on the sign outside the entrance.

Over the next two hours, Uncle Peter showed Akimbo every corner of the park. He showed him the enclosure, with its trees and branches set out to give the snakes a natural habitat. He showed him the special cages, dimly lit, each containing one or two snakes. He showed him the small laboratory, where there were snakes preserved in bottles, coiled and lifeless, but still looking as if at any moment they could spring out of the bottles. Then there was a collection of snake eggs, all neatly labeled with information about the species and when and where the egg was found.

It was all every bit as interesting as Akimbo had expected, and the time passed very quickly. At midmorning, Uncle Peter looked at his watch. "Milking time already," he said. "I almost forgot."

Akimbo was puzzled. *Milking time?* Did they keep a cow or a goat somewhere? Did they feed milk to the snakes? Surely not.

Uncle Peter saw his nephew's confusion and laughed heartily.

"No, not that sort of milking!" he said. "We milk the snakes for their venom. Haven't you heard about it?"

Akimbo shook his head. He thought that he knew about snakes, but it was obvious that he had a lot to learn.

"Come," said Uncle Peter. "I'll go and fetch one of my assistants."

They went to the edge of the enclosure,

where there was a special gate, which enabled the staff to go in. The assistant was already standing there, waiting for Uncle Peter. As his uncle arrived, the assistant handed him a list. Uncle Peter looked at it for a few moments, and then nodded.

"We're going to milk two cobras today," he said to Akimbo. "One of them is a banded cobra, the other a king cobra. They're big snakes."

Akimbo peered over the edge of the enclosure wall, with its natural habitat filled with snakes. Down below he could see a large snake lying on a patch of grass, almost immobile apart from the flicking of its forked tongue. Uncle Peter followed his nephew's gaze.

"He uses that tongue of his to smell things," he explained. "He's not sticking his tongue out at anybody! But he's not the one we want to see."

Uncle Peter spoke for a few moments to his assistant and then told Akimbo to join a small group of visitors standing beside the wall.

"We let visitors to the park watch this," he said. "It gives them a bit of excitement."

As Akimbo went and stood beside the band of visitors, Uncle Peter and his assistant let themselves into the enclosure. Akimbo held his breath as his uncle made his way toward the other side; the whole place seemed to be teeming with snakes. What if he stepped on one, or one of them decided to attack him? Surely his uncle knew exactly what he was doing, but Akimbo still could not help feeling worried.

Suddenly Uncle Peter and his assistant stopped. The assistant had been carrying a long pole with what looked like a clip of some sort at one end and a lever at the other. Uncle Peter took the pole from his assistant and very slowly advanced on a large snake that was sunning itself no more than a few paces away.

It seemed as if the snake was unaware of the men's presence. Akimbo watched as his uncle inched his way toward it. Was the snake asleep, or did it just not care? Perhaps it was tame, like the snakes that snake charmers carry in their baskets.

Suddenly, the snake uncoiled itself, and its head darted forward and up. Akimbo drew

in his breath. There, swaying before his uncle, with its cobra's hood fanned out, was one of the most dangerous snakes in Africa. Uncle Peter stood very still. He did not seem in the least bit worried about the snake, and with a sudden movement of his arm, he pushed the pole forward and pinned the snake's head to the ground. Then, pressing gently at the lever, he closed the jaws of the pole around the snake, just below its head.

The rest of the snake was not at all happy about what was happening. The body and tail lashed backward and forward as the angry snake attempted to wriggle free from the restraint. At a signal from Uncle Peter, the assistant stepped forward and grasped the tail of the snake firmly in his hand. Then the two men lifted up their captive and carried him writhing toward the wall where the observers were standing.

Another assistant had appeared and took Uncle Peter's place while handing him a small glass jar. Uncle Peter stepped forward and spoke to the people staring over the low wall of the enclosure.

"This jar," he explained, "has a thin plastic membrane stretched over its top, like a plastic bag. I am now going to push the snake's fangs through this and force it to eject its venom—its poison—into the jar. That's what we call 'milking a snake.'"

"But why do you do it?" somebody asked. "Isn't it bad for the snake?"

Uncle Peter smiled. "They may not like it very much, but it does them no harm. And as to why we do it, we collect the venom for laboratories that make serums to treat snake bites. You need the venom if you want to make medicine to cure snake bites. That's why we do it."

He turned away and walked to the assistant holding the pole. Then, very carefully, Uncle Peter took hold of the snake just behind its head and held it firmly between his thumb and forefinger. The jaws of the snake-catching pole were released, and the snake's head was held over the jar.

Akimbo saw that the snake's mouth was now open, and two wicked-looking curled fangs were exposed. Uncle Peter forced the head down, and the fangs pierced the membrane on top of the jar. With another finger, he pressed the top of the snake's head, and out came the venom—pure, clear drops of deadly poison—ejected through holes at the end of those vicious fangs. The crowd held its breath as the milking took place. There was not much venom to harvest, no more than a teaspoonful perhaps, but Akimbo knew it was more than enough to kill a fully grown man.

With the milking over, Uncle Peter held the snake away from him. At his command, both he and his assistant let go of the reptile, tossing it safely away from them. The snake shot off, indignant and confused, and they in the meantime went off to find their next victim.

The milking of the second cobra was a quicker affair, as there was no explanation and the snake was a bit smaller. Then, with that snake released, Uncle Peter pocketed the two jars of venom and left the enclosure.

Akimbo joined his uncle's side as they made their way to the laboratory.

"We've got to get this into the fridge as

soon as possible," said Uncle Peter. "It's of no use if we let it spoil."

In the laboratory, each jar was carefully labeled and stored in a large refrigerator in the corner of the room. There were many other jars there, all similarly labeled, all awaiting collection by the people who make the snake-bite serum. Now it was lunchtime, and Akimbo and his uncle sat down to eat a sandwich in his uncle's small office. It was a comfortable room, cool and secluded, and filled with books and pictures of snakes.

"Just about anything that you could want to find out about snakes is here," said Uncle Peter proudly. "But, all in all, experience with snakes is the best way to find out about them."

He handed Akimbo a chart with pictures of many different snakes on it. "You can have that," he said. "You never know when it might be useful."

Akimbo looked at the pictures. There were quite a few snakes on it that he very much hoped he would never have to meet!

MOST DANGEROUS

That afternoon, Uncle Peter showed Akimbo the work that he had in mind for him while he was staying at the snake park. It was a job that used to be done by an old man who loved snakes, but he had decided to retire and go and live with his sons in the country. The job was feeding some of the snakes in the cages and writing down what they ate.

"We like to know if a snake is eating or not," said Uncle Peter. "So we keep a note of what they get and when they eat it."

It was not a difficult job to do, and Akimbo was delighted to be given the responsibility. Some of the snakes ate lizards, and he had to catch the lizards from the tank where they were kept and then drop them into the right cage. At first it seemed cruel to Akimbo, and he felt sorry for the lizards, but then he remembered that this was exactly what snakes would eat in nature, and the snakes couldn't go hungry.

The snakes seemed to pay no attention to the lizard when first it was dropped into the cage, but later when Akimbo returned, the lizard had often disappeared and the snake looked fatter and was sleeping. Feeding the very large snakes, particularly the pythons, was a more difficult business. These snakes ate rabbits or rats, and they were slower in swallowing their larger prey than the smaller snakes.

Over the next few days, Akimbo got used to his job in the snake park, and was pleased when Uncle Peter congratulated him.

"You're doing very well!" he said. "But remember one thing: no matter how confident you get, bear in mind that some snakes are just waiting for you to get careless. And with some of these snakes, you'll never get a chance to get careless again!"

Akimbo took the advice to heart. He knew that many of the snakes in the park could inflict a fatal bite, and he was determined never to get too close to them. He was not allowed in the enclosure, of course, and he was also forbidden to feed one or two of the very aggressive or very dangerous snakes— this was done by Uncle Peter—but he was still careful to check that a snake was at the other end of the cage when he opened the feeding hatch to toss in its food.

One of the men who worked at the park, Luke, had been bitten very seriously by a puff adder a couple of years ago and told Akimbo all about it.

"That's the sort of snake that bit me," he said, pointing to a thick, fairly short snake that lay lazily at the end of the enclosure.

Akimbo looked at the puff adder. He knew a little bit about these snakes. Unlike many other snakes, which would get out of people's way before anybody got at all close to them,

these snakes were sluggish. They would lie in the grass and the first you knew of them was when you heard them hissing as you were on the point of stepping on them.

"I didn't see it," Luke said. "I could have sworn it wasn't there. I was picking up another snake for milking, and I took a step backward, right onto the end of a puff adder.

"It gave a tremendous hiss, and then twisted itself around, and latched onto my leg. They have terrible fangs, those snakes. They hook onto you and pump in the venom.

"Oddly enough, it wasn't painful right at the beginning. I pulled him off and ran to the gate. Then I felt it begin to sting."

Luke grimaced as he remembered the incident. "Your uncle was in his office, but he ran to the laboratory more quickly than I had ever seen him move before. We keep the anti-venom there, you see. It had to be kept cool.

"He came back and filled the syringe before my eyes. Then he injected me all around the bite and gave me another injection farther up my leg. By now my leg was throbbing with pain, and it felt as if somebody were running a hot knife into it. I tried to walk, but it was too painful, and so they had to carry me out to the truck.

"I hardly remember the trip to the hospital. I think I fainted, because the next thing I knew, I was in the hospital and a doctor was feeling my leg. I gave a shout each time his hands touched my flesh—it was that painful.

"I spent a month in the hospital altogether. I was lucky. If I hadn't had those injections straight away, it could have been much worse."

Akimbo listened to the story quietly. "Next time I'm walking through the park," he thought, "I'll take special care where I put my feet."

But it was not the puff adders that were the most dangerous snakes in the snake park. This honor—if you could call it that— belonged to two other species, which were very different to look at but both were extremely dangerous.

The first of these was the Gaboon Viper. This was a thick diamond-patterned snake, which Akimbo was not allowed to feed. It was not all that long, but it made up for its lack of length by being almost as thick as a python. At one end it had a curious, spade-shaped head, in which two dark black eyes glittered. At the other end, its body tapered abruptly to a thin tail.

The Gaboon Viper was a beautiful snake to look at. The diamond pattern on its spine was yellow and green and looked like fallen leaves. This was no accident: this snake liked to live in forests, and the leaflike pattern of its skin provided the perfect camouflage.

"The problem with a bite from the Gaboon Viper," said Akimbo's uncle, "is that we just don't have an anti-venom to deal with it. The normal injections would be almost useless if you were bitten by one."

The other extremely dangerous snake was more common, and more widely dreaded, throughout that part of Africa. This was the mamba, a name that in Akimbo's mind spelled danger.

"There are two sorts of mamba," explained Uncle Peter. "The black mamba is the more common sort, and we've got them here. The other is the green mamba, which many people say is even more dangerous than its black cousin."

"Why is that?" asked Akimbo. "Is its poison stronger?"

"No, it's weaker," answered Uncle Peter. "But the green mamba lives in trees, you see. It has been known to drop down on people walking below them. The black mamba is usually on the ground, where you can see it."

Uncle Peter took Akimbo to the mamba cage. Inside, two long black snakes moved slowly over the twigs of a branch. The snakes watched Akimbo through the glass of the cage, their eyes unflickering, their small forked tongues darting in and out in rapid, almost invisible movements.

The sight of the two snakes chilled Akimbo. There was something sinister about them, and he imagined what it would be like to be chased by an angry black mamba. He had heard that a snake like that could outpace a person over a short distance, and if this happened, you had very little chance of escape.

"What would happen if one of them bit you?" he asked Uncle Peter.

His uncle was silent for a few moments. "Many people say you'd last about four minutes," he said. "That may be true, or it may not. I think you'd be very lucky to survive, though."

The snakes moved suddenly, and one of them slid right up to the glass front of the cage and stared at Akimbo. Akimbo drew back, and his uncle laughed.

"Don't worry," he said. "They're perfectly safe—as long as they're in there, and you're out here!"

Akimbo noticed that the next cage was empty. "What was in there?" he asked.

Uncle Peter tapped the glass of the empty cage.

"That cage is reserved," he said. "I've been waiting for a green mamba for years now, but I've never managed to catch one. The day I do, it goes in there!"

MAMBA HUNT

kimbo remembered his promise to his father and wrote a letter home. He told his parents how much he was enjoying staying with Uncle Peter, and he described everything that his uncle had arranged for him to do. He had been to a movie with Uncle Peter, and he had made new friends. But most of all, he told them about the snake park and the snakes he had seen.

Uncle Peter now found a few more duties for his nephew. As well as feeding, Akimbo was allowed to handle some of the less dangerous snakes. This was a particular thrill for him, and one of his proudest moments was when he had been allowed to display a small python to a group of visiting schoolchildren. Akimbo had taken the snake out of its cage, making sure to hold it firmly behind its head, just as his uncle had taught him. Since it was still young, the python was only the length of Akimbo's arm, but Akimbo was surprised at its strength. As he displayed it, the snake wound its body around his wrist and forearm. Akimbo felt the power of its muscles underneath the cool, supple skin.

There were other excitements, too. He was allowed to hold the jar for the milking of a cobra—his hand shook a bit at first, but he soon became used to it. He was allowed to carry a harmless grass snake around in his pocket, and in the afternoons, when there was not a great deal to do, Akimbo would sit in his uncle's office and read about snakes. He could identify just about every snake in the park now, and his uncle was proud of him.

Then came the call that Uncle Peter had waited so long to get. It came in the morning, when Akimbo was feeding the snakes, and the first thing he knew of it was his uncle shouting for him from his office. Akimbo ran to see what he wanted. He found Uncle Peter standing behind his desk, his eyes bright with excitement.

"Something very interesting has happened," his uncle announced. "I've just had a phone call from a policeman out in a little village. They're having trouble with a snake, and from what they say about it, I think it may be what we're looking for!"

Akimbo caught his breath. "A green mamba?" he asked.

Uncle Peter smiled. "I think so," he said. "Sometimes people exaggerate, and I go off looking for something that turns out to be a grass snake, or something like that. But I've got a feeling about this one."

Uncle Peter told Akimbo what to do. He was to finish with his feeding duties, and then they would go back to the house to fetch a few things. "We could be away for a few days," he said. "You'll need some more clothes, and I'll also have to get my tent. But, with any luck, we can be on our way within two hours."

*   *   *

It took slightly longer than that, but at last they set off to the village that had reported the snake. It was a long journey, almost three hours. Akimbo dozed as they traveled, only to be woken by bumps in the untarred road. There had been strong rains recently, and some of the road had washed away in parts. But Uncle Peter was used to driving in the bush, and he managed to avoid the worst of the potholes.

They almost drove straight past the village, it was so small. It was more of a settlement, really, with a few brick buildings and the rest of the houses made out of compacted mud. The people were farmers, with a few crops and rather thin cattle. It was not a rich part of the country, but people seemed happy enough and nobody seemed to want for food.

Uncle Peter parked the truck under the shade of a thorn tree, and they made their way over to one of the brick buildings, which seemed to be the police post, and found the policeman sitting inside. He welcomed them heartily and gave them a drink of water.

"It was good of you to call me," said Uncle Peter. "Some people don't bother."

The policeman smiled. "I visited your snake park once," he said. "It was quite a long time ago, but I remember reading your advice about how you relied on people to help you find snakes."

The policeman rose to his feet and called to somebody outside the window. A few minutes later, two boys no older than Akimbo were standing at the door waiting to be invited in by the policeman.

The policeman beckoned them in. "These are the boys who saw the snake," he said. "They can tell you the story themselves."

The two boys looked shy; their gaze fixed on the floor.

"Don't be frightened," said Uncle Peter gently. "You just tell me what you saw."

There was silence for a few moments. Then one of the boys spoke. "We were herding goats," he said. "Up that way, near the hills. Some of the goats had wandered into the trees, and we went in to find them. There's a place there where there's a cave.

There's a small stream, and many, many high trees." The boy stopped.

"Go on," said Uncle Peter. "What happened then?"

The boy looked up. "We were walking near the stream, when suddenly I heard a noise in front of me. There was one of goats, and it was on its front legs, crying. Then it fell down and rolled over. I ran up to it, and then I saw the snake shoot off. It was a long, long green one, with a head like this."

The boy made a diamond shape with his two hands. As he saw this, Uncle Peter nodded his head enthusiastically.

"Was it a dark green or a light green?" he asked.

The boy thought for a moment. "It was a light green."

"And then?" prodded Uncle Peter. "What happened then?"

"The snake made for a hole nearby and went down that," said the boy. "I put a stick in the ground so that we would remember where it happened."

"Well done," said Uncle Peter.

The policeman now chimed in. "This is the second animal that has died near there," he said. "A cow was bitten, and now this goat. The people cannot afford to lose these animals."

"I understand," said Uncle Peter.

"And they are afraid," said the policeman. "They want me to kill this snake."

"I am glad you called me," said Uncle Peter quickly. "It's not a good thing to kill snakes. It serves no purpose."

"What will you do?" asked the policeman.

"I'll try to catch this snake," replied Uncle Peter. "If it's a green mamba, then I will be very happy to take him back to the snake park."

The two men discussed their plan, while Akimbo went out to talk to the two herd boys. A short while later, Uncle Peter appeared and called Akimbo over to him.

"We're going to set up our tent," he said. "Then, first thing tomorrow morning, the boys will take us to where they saw the snake."

Akimbo enjoyed camping. He helped Uncle

Peter erect the tent, and together they made sure that everything was ready for the next morning. That evening, they ate with the people of the village, and there was much talk of snakes. Everybody had something to say, including one old man who claimed to have seen a python that had swallowed a fully grown donkey. Uncle Peter doubted this and later told Akimbo that it was impossible, but he did not interrupt the old man in his story.

Akimbo was so excited that he found it difficult to sleep that night. As he lay in the tent, with the sounds of the African night and the scrunch of the night insects ringing in his ears, he imagined what it would be like to look for the green mamba the following day. He expected to dream of snakes, but he did not, or, if he did, he did not remember his dreams.

The next day, after breakfast, they set off on foot with the two herd boys. At first, they followed a footpath, but this gave out after a while and the boys led them through bush that became thicker and thicker. Akimbo saw hills in the distance, and he guessed that this was where they were heading, but even after they had been walking for several hours, the hills seemed as far away as ever.

They paused at one point and rested under the shade of a wide-branched tree. Then they set off again, moving through bush that became thicker and thicker. At last, after walking for almost two hours more, they arrived at a place where the ground began to slope up toward the hills.

"We are nearly there," said one of the boys, pointing ahead of them. "That is the place."

He pointed to a spot where the broad granite rocks of the hill divided to make a tree-filled cleft. Akimbo saw the place where the stream appeared, and there, on the bank nearest them, was a stick pushed into the ground.

It was now time for Uncle Peter to take control. He told the herd boys to go back to the waiting place and stay there. He and

Akimbo remained where they were, Akimbo holding a stout canvas bag that his uncle had taken out of his knapsack. Uncle Peter busied himself with assembling a collapsible metal pole, very similar to the ones used to catch snakes in the snake park. Then, signaling to Akimbo to keep quiet, he led the way slowly along the bank. The herd boys had said that the hole into which the snake disappeared was only a short distance away from the stick. Akimbo and his uncle strained their eyes to make out a hole in the bank, but they could find none. Then Akimbo gave a start. There, virtually beneath his feet, was a hole in the ground, smooth and well used—a snake hole!

Akimbo moved back instinctively, and Uncle Peter spun around. For a moment, Uncle Peter seemed angry, as he had told Akimbo not to make any sound or sudden movements. But when he saw what Akimbo was pointing at, he nodded his understanding and moved back himself.

"We can wait over there," he whispered,

nodding to an old termite heap projecting out of the grass behind them. "We can watch the hole from there."

Gently, trying to walk as softly as possible, Akimbo and his uncle moved back from the snake's lair. Now the waiting was to begin.

CAPTURE!

The sun moved slowly overhead, making the shadows shorter and then lengthening them again. In the bush around the two watching figures, nothing moved, although in the trees around them now and then a bird fluttered from branch to branch. Akimbo wondered whether it was worth waiting. The snake could be anywhere—it could even have moved from the hole and established a refuge elsewhere. If this had happened, they would spend hours and hours beside an empty hole in the ground, waiting for a snake that would never come.

Then something caught Akimbo's eye. At first he thought he was imagining it, but then he realized he was not. There was a movement just within the hole. Yes, something was there.

Uncle Peter saw it, too. "That's it," he whispered to Akimbo. "Now watch."

Slowly a head moved out of the hole, followed by a section of lithe, thin snake's body. Akimbo felt Uncle Peter stiffen beside him.

"Mamba," his uncle whispered, almost under his breath. "They were right."

Akimbo hardly dared breathe. The snake, as it emerged from the hole, showed itself to be immensely long, at least twice his own height. He glanced at his uncle, wondering what he intended to do. Would he really try to chase that? Uncle Peter gestured to Akimbo to stay where he was. Then, rising to his feet, he began to move slowly toward the snake.

The mamba seemed unaware of Uncle Peter's approach, lying seemingly inert on the ground in front of the hole. Akimbo saw a large fly land on one of the snake's coils, and this made it twitch, but only slightly. Uncle Peter had the extended pole held out before him. He was now sufficiently close to the snake for the jaws of the pole to be hovering almost around the snake's body.

"Now," thought Akimbo. "Now's your chance."

It may have been the shadow thrown by the pole, or it may have been some tremor in the ground that alerted the snake. Whatever it was, the head of the snake suddenly whipped around to confront the danger. For a moment, the deadly reptile and its pursuer faced one another, but then in a sudden flash, the snake shot away, flying up the bank like an arrow released from a bow.

Uncle Peter gave a cry and began to follow the snake, holding the pole up against his chest. Akimbo sprang to his feet and followed his uncle.

"Watch him!" called out Uncle Peter. "See where he goes!"

Akimbo knew how easy it was to lose sight of a fleeing snake, so he was not surprised when the snake seemed to vanish completely into a dense clump of trees.

Uncle Peter stopped and waited for Akimbo to catch up with him. "Did you see where it went?" he asked, the disappointment clearly showing in his voice.

Akimbo pointed to the place where he had last seen the snake. "I think it was in there," he said.

Uncle Peter nodded. "I suspect it's gone," he said. "But there's no harm in our just checking up on those trees to see if it's gone up one of them."

They approached the clump of trees gingerly. At any moment, the snake could reappear. Mambas were aggressive—Akimbo had read that time and time again. They could stand their ground and attack when other snakes would think only of seeking out safety. Now they were entering the mamba's territory. It was the one that knew the trees, not them. They were the ones who were weak and vulnerable in such terrain.

There were about ten or twelve trees in the clump, and Uncle Peter said they should work their way through, looking carefully at every branch. "It may look like a twig up there," he warned. "Look for curves rather than straight lines—that's how you spot a snake in a tree."

Akimbo looked at the first tree, holding his hand above his eyes as he peered at each branch. The foliage was dense, and the leaves provided good cover. His heart sank; it was a hopeless task. He stopped. Was that something? Did that branch move? He looked again. No, it was the wind in the leaves—there was nothing there.

They moved farther into the trees. In the back of his mind, Akimbo remembered the warning about green mambas falling from trees onto their victims below. The thought made his flesh creep.

They checked up on several more trees, each time without result. But they knew that they could have walked right past the mamba in such conditions. He could have been in any one of dozens of thick clusters of leaves, immobile, save for the flickering tongue, watching silently. Perhaps he would even track them. Snakes had been known to do that.

Suddenly Akimbo stopped. There was something strange about that branch, he was sure of it. He peered at it again. There was a fork in the branch, and then several twigs.

There were leaves, some of them green, some ready to fall. And then . . . he stood absolutely still. There was a movement on the branch, and just below it, the shape of a coil of snake. Then that moved, too.

Akimbo looked around him. Uncle Peter was standing a little distance away, looking up into a tree. Akimbo put his fingers to his mouth and gave a quiet whistle. It could have been a bird, or a cicada, but his uncle turned around and looked at him inquisitively.

Akimbo mouthed the words "Up there!" and pointed at the branch.

Uncle Peter raised a hand in acknowledgment and moved quickly over to his nephew's side. "Where?" he whispered.

Akimbo pointed again, and after a few moments Uncle Peter spotted the snake as well.

"Right," he said. "I'm going up after it."

Akimbo was shocked. "Surely you won't go up . . . there," he protested. "It's too dangerous."

Uncle Peter brushed aside his objection. "I can get quite close to that branch if I go up

to where the trunk divides," he said. "Then my pole should be able to reach him."

Akimbo stood back as his uncle began to climb up the tree. As he did so, Akimbo watched the snake, waiting to see if it moved. It was quite still. Slowly, painfully slowly, it seemed to Akimbo, Uncle Peter inched his way up the tree. When he reached the point where the main trunk of the tree divided, he stopped and steadied himself. Then the pole began to move out slowly toward the mamba.

Akimbo watched, fascinated and terrified at the same time. The snake was still moving, but only slightly, and it seemed to Akimbo that even if the snake sensed their presence, it felt safe on the leafy branch. Once again, Uncle Peter moved the pole in a deft downward thrust, and this time it fell upon the snake and the jaws clasped tight.

There was a whipping and thrashing commotion of snake and leaves. Then there seemed to be no more movement, and Akimbo wondered whether the snake was truly caught. But then Uncle Peter called out, triumphant, and began to work his way down the tree, bringing the pole behind him.

"I've got him," he said. "Get the bag ready."

Akimbo unfolded the large canvas bag and made sure that the strings that drew the mouth tight were untangled. Then Uncle Peter was down from the tree, bearing at the end of his pole the long angry body of the captured snake.

As Akimbo watched, Uncle Peter moved his grip on the pole higher. Then when he was close enough, he reached forward with his free hand and seized the snake's tail. Now it was ready for bagging. Akimbo held the mouth of the bag wide open, while Uncle Peter pushed in the end of the pole holding the snake just below the head. Once that was inside, he thrust the rest of the snake's squirming body into the bag and drew the strings at the mouth tight around the pole.

"Now," he said, "I'll release the clasp and pull out the pole. The moment that happens, pull the strings tight. But don't touch the bag itself."

Akimbo did as he was told. As soon as the jaws of the pole appeared, he pulled the strings as tight as he could. Uncle Peter then took them from him and knotted them. The bag itself collapsed, although there were signs of fierce movement within as the snake struggled vainly against the confines of its prison.

Uncle Peter sat down and wiped his brow. "That went well!" he said, smiling at his nephew. "Thank you."

A Brush with Danger

The two herd boys had been waiting patiently, and now rushed out to greet Akimbo and his uncle as soon as they saw them come out of the trees. They both looked at the canvas sack, which Uncle Peter was carrying carefully before him.

"Is it in there?" the elder of the two boys asked. "Is that the snake?"

Uncle Peter nodded his reply.

"We caught it in a tree," said Akimbo. "Or rather, my uncle caught it in a tree."

"We both did," said Uncle Peter. "It was Akimbo who saw it."

They walked back to the village, the journey seeming to take far less time now that they had completed their task. When they arrived, people crowded around, looking fearfully at the bulging snake sack.

"The boys were right," said Uncle Peter. "It was a green mamba."

"We don't want such snakes," one man said. "They are evil."

Uncle Peter shook his head sadly. "No," he said. "You're wrong. No snake is evil. It has its job to do. If you had no snakes, your crops would all be eaten by rats. Did you know that?"

While Uncle Peter talked to the policeman, who was very proud of having arranged for the snake to be caught, Akimbo took down the tent and packed it neatly away in the back of the truck. Then they said goodbye, and Uncle Peter carefully placed the canvas bag in the back of the truck as well, resting it on the folded tent to protect the body of the snake from jolts and jars on the rough road back. Halfway back, they stopped at a small gas station beside the road. It was a desolate spot, surrounded by trees, and with a wide plain stretching in every direction. The gas station was also a store, selling food to travelers and to the people of nearby settlements. Once the truck was filled up with gas, Uncle Peter went with the attendant to collect his change and buy a snack for the rest of the journey. Akimbo stayed in the truck, as it was hot outside, and he was feeling tired.

There was a noise, a soft, almost rustling noise, as if a locust or a bird had landed on top of the truck. Akimbo wondered what it was, but paid no further attention to it. Then in a sudden, awful moment he saw the snake's head and body sliding smoothly over the back of Uncle Peter's seat and into the cabin of the truck.

Every detail of that moment would be etched in Akimbo's mind. He saw the sharp, glowing green of the snake's skin, the myriad of interwoven scales; he saw the snake's neatly shaped head, its eyes within their protective membrane, the fine nostrils, and the small tight mouth that concealed those terrible deadly fangs.

Akimbo stayed absolutely still; his body

frozen with terror, every nerve shrieking a warning. He knew that if he moved now, the snake would strike, and he would die. The snake slid its long body over the seat and down onto the floor of the truck. Akimbo turned his eyes slowly downward; the snake seemed to be twining itself around the brake pedal and the clutch. Now it moved again, and Akimbo felt a soft, brushing touch against his bare leg and foot. The snake was on his feet!

The snake stopped. Perhaps it liked the warmth of his skin; perhaps it had come to the limit of its exploring and was now content to wait. Akimbo made a supreme effort to stay still. His skin crawled with pinlike sensations of terror; his heart thumped within him like a hammer. But he willed himself to remain very still, and he succeeded.

He looked outside, turning his head as gently as he could. Uncle Peter was exchanging a few words with the attendant, cracking a joke. *Come!* willed Akimbo. *Come now!*

Uncle Peter turned away and began to walk back to the truck. Akimbo now had to

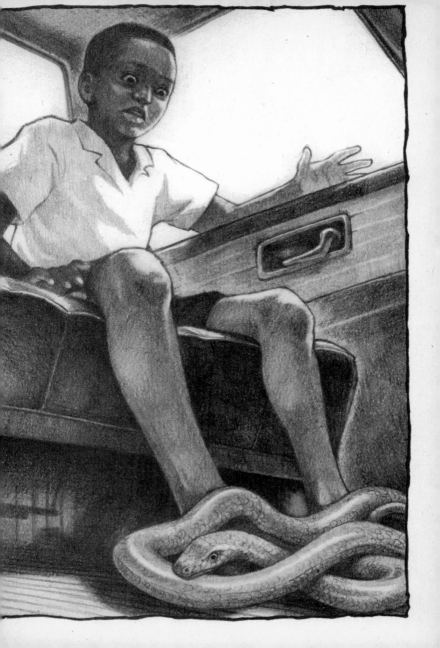

think quickly. It was vital that he alert his uncle before he opened the truck door—a disturbance of that nature would prompt the snake to strike, either at Akimbo or at his uncle. And yet, Akimbo would also disturb the snake if he shouted or moved quickly.

Akimbo decided what he had to do. He took a deep breath, and very slowly, like a figure in a slow-motion film, he began to move his arm. The snake remained still. Then, keeping the rest of his body immobile, Akimbo moved his arm out of the truck and waved to his uncle.

Uncle Peter waved back. Akimbo, desperate now, shook his hand up and down and pointed. Uncle Peter appeared not to notice, then he suddenly stopped. Akimbo responded by pointing again to the inside of the truck. Then he shook his arm again.

Uncle Peter was puzzled. He hesitated for a moment, and then he began to approach Akimbo's side of the truck. As he came nearer, he saw from the way the boy was sitting that something was wrong.

"The mamba," whispered Akimbo once

Uncle Peter was close enough. "It's escaped. It's in here—on my feet."

Uncle Peter seemed to reel from the shock. Then he moved slightly closer, stepping carefully to avoid making any noise or vibration. "Stay absolutely still," he whispered. "Try not to move at all. I'm going to go around to fetch my pole from the back. Then I'm going to try to open my door very, very gently. But you mustn't do anything at all. Do you understand?"

"Yes," whispered Akimbo. "But please hurry, Uncle."

Uncle Peter disappeared around the back of the truck, and Akimbo thought that he heard the faintest of sounds from behind him, but the snake did not move. Now Uncle Peter appeared at the driver's side window. He peered in, trying to see where the snake was lying, but it was dark down there, and he could not make out its shape.

Akimbo watched in an agony of suspense as Uncle Peter very slowly pushed down on the handle of the driver's door. A chink of light appeared between the frame of the door and the body of the truck and grew larger as the door was opened, fraction by fraction. Every part of Akimbo's body now ached with the effort of keeping still. He would have given anything to flex his muscles and move, but he knew that the slightest movement on his part could set the snake into a fury.

Opening the door seemed to take an eternity, but at last, the chink of light widened, then flooded into the cabin of the truck. "Surely the snake would move now," thought Akimbo. Its escape route was clear; it would have no reason to stay.

For a few minutes, the snake did nothing, and Akimbo's heart sank. What if it had come to stay? What if it liked it where it was? He could not stay still indefinitely—sooner or later his protesting muscles would have to flex.

Then the snake moved. Akimbo heard a rustling movement, and suddenly he felt the pressure come off his foot. From the corner of his eye, he saw an unfolding of green coils, and with a sinuous gliding action, the snake eased across the floor of the cab and out of the truck. Uncle Peter was standing to the side of the truck, and the snake did not see him as it slid down onto the ground. The next thing it knew was the cold grip of the jaws of the pole, tight around its throat. It was caught again.

"You are very brave," said Uncle Peter as they prepared to leave. "You did just the right thing in keeping still. It's when people panic that snakes lash out. They don't like sudden movements."

Akimbo accepted the praise. He had done his best, but he hoped that it would be a long time before he was called upon to be brave again!

"How did it escape?" asked Akimbo.

"My fault, I'm afraid," said Uncle Peter. "I can't have tied up the bag tightly enough. I won't make that mistake again!"

They continued on their journey. Uncle Peter was concerned that Akimbo had been so frightened by his experience that he would lose all interest in snakes. But this was not to be. Once they returned to the snake park, Akimbo was eager to watch the green mamba being settled into its new home. He did not mind either when a reporter from the local newspaper, a friend of Uncle Peter, came to talk to him about the incident. And after they had talked, the photographer from the newspaper took a photograph of Akimbo standing in front of the cage containing the very same snake.

Akimbo was very proud to see his photograph and packed a copy of the newspaper in his bag to show his parents when he got home. *"Boy and snake come face to face,"* said the newspaper report, *"in a truck!"*

And then it was time to leave. Akimbo wished he could stay with his uncle much longer, as he still had a lot to learn about snakes. But there was school to get back to, and things to learn there, too.

He said good-bye sadly to Uncle Peter at the bus station.

"Thank you," he said. "These have been the most interesting weeks of my life."

Uncle Peter smiled. "You'll be back," he said. "Now that we've trained you, you'll have to come back next school vacation."

"I will," said Akimbo.

And he did. When he returned six months later, for his next working vacation with Uncle Peter, the first snake he looked at in the snake park was the green mamba. The snake was in good condition, which pleased Akimbo, but what made him happier than anything else was to see his name on the label below the cage. CAUGHT BY AKIMBO, it said, and then the date. Akimbo beamed with pride. This was better, far better, than any other thanks.

Did You Know?

• There are approximately 2,500 known snake species. Twenty percent of that total number are considered poisonous.

• Snakes live in oceans, trees, and on the land, and it is believed that they evolved from lizards.

• Snakes are deaf, but they are able to pick up vibrations in their jawbones, and their tongues can detect scent molecules.

• Snakes find their prey by sight, scent, and sometimes temperature. Their sense of smell is extraordinary. By constantly flicking their forked tongues, they carry scent particles to a specialized sensory organ ("Jacobson's organ") on the roof of the mouth. Some snakes even have infrared receptors in the deep grooves between their nostrils and eyes that allow them to "see" the radiated heat of their prey.

• Snakes move by using special muscles attached to their ribs. The scales on their bellies also act as anchors. The fastest recorded speed achieved by any snake is about eight miles per hour, but few can move that fast.

• Unlike eels, sea snakes have no gills and must rise to the surface for air. They can remain underwater for several hours, obtaining dissolved oxygen from water that they swallow and eject.

• Three species of snake can spit, or eject, their venom in a fine spray, which can be projected for distances up to eight feet. If the venom gets into the eyes, it may cause blindness. The spitting is used only in defense.

- The snake responsible for the most human deaths is the saw-scaled or carpet viper (*Echis carinatus*). Ranging from West Africa to India, it bites and kills more people in the world than any other species.

- The longest fangs of any snake are those of the highly venomous Gaboon viper (*Bitis gabonica*). In a specimen six feet long, the fangs measured two inches.

- The Gaboon viper also produces the most venom. Thanks to its two-inch-long fangs, this creature also injects its poison deeper than any other snake! Although generally sluggish by nature, Gaboon vipers are unpredictable and capable of great speed in short bursts, making them extremely dangerous.

- The longest snake is the reticulated python (*Python reticulatus*), of Southeast Asia, Indonesia, and the Philippines, regularly exceeding twenty feet six inches. The record length is thirty-two feet nine-and-a-half inches, for a specimen found in Celebes, Indonesia, in 1912.

• Snakes played an important role in Egyptian history. The Nile cobra adorned the crown of the pharaohs. It was even worshipped as one of the gods. Cobras were also used for sinister purposes, such as murdering an enemy.

AFRICAN WILDLIFE FOUNDATION®

You can learn all about elephants and
lions and cheetahs and zebras and
giraffes and other wildlife by visiting the
African Wildlife Foundation at
www.awf.org.

After you learn about the wild animals,
you can help save them—by supporting
the African Wildlife Foundation.

The African Wildlife Foundation has
worked with the people of Africa for
forty-five years. They train park rangers,
like Akimbo's father, to protect wildlife
and catch poachers. They give scholar-
ships to girls and boys like Akimbo so
they can grow up and learn to be scien-
tists who protect Africa's mighty rivers
and great forests.

A Note on the Author

ALEXANDER McCALL SMITH has written more than fifty books, including the *New York Times* bestselling No. 1 Ladies' Detective Agency mysteries and The Sunday Philosophy Club series. A professor of medical law at Edinburgh University, he was born in what is now Zimbabwe and taught law at the University of Botswana. He lives in Edinburgh, Scotland.

Visit him at WWW.ALEXANDERMCCALLSMITH.COM

A Note on the Illustrator

LEUYEN PHAM is the illustrator of numerous award-winning books for children including *Big Sister, Little Sister* (which she also wrote); *Sing-Along Song; Piggies in a Polka;* and *Freckleface Strawberry*. She lives in San Francisco, California.

Visit her at WWW.LEUYENPHAM.COM

Don't miss any adventure

mystery, and fun with these

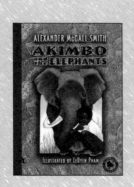

Alexander McCall Smith titles!